IVY

FLEDERMAUS

BOSUN

SKIPPER

There is a lot of tiny text on this page and the
Adventuremice were wondering if you would read it.
If you have read it: congratulations!
You have keen eyes and would make an
excellent member of our Adventuremice team.
You can find out more about what we get up
to on our website: Adventuremice.com

THIS BOOK IS DEDICATED TO THE
BOVEY TRACEY BELL RINGERS

Adventuremice: Mice on the Ice
is a
DAVID FICKLING BOOK

First published in Great Britain in 2023 by David Fickling Books,
31 Beaumont Street, Oxford, OX1 2NP
www.davidficklingbooks.com

Text © Philip Reeve & Sarah McIntyre, 2023
Illustrations © Sarah McIntyre, 2023

978-1-78845-269-4

WEST NORTHAMPTONSHIRE COUNCIL		
60000536460		
Askews & Holts		
DD		

ADVENTUREMICE
MICE ON THE ICE

BY PHILIP REEVE & SARAH McINTYRE

d·b
David Fickling Books

'SNOW!' shouted Fledermaus, crashing into Pedro's bedroom early one winter's morning. 'It has SNOWED, Pedro! Let's go outside!'

'Snow?' Pedro peeked out from under the covers. Before he came to stay with Fledermaus and the other Adventuremice at their Mousebase he had lived under the floorboards of Hilltop House, and none of his family had ever gone outside when it snowed. They had made mugs of hot chocolate and curled up in their nests and snoozed until all the nasty stuff had melted. But here was Fledermaus, all wrapped up in scarf and mittens, absolutely itching to get out in the snow. And from outside the window Pedro could hear the shouts and laughter of the other Adventuremice . . .

It sounded as if they were having fun.

So Pedro scrambled out of his nest,

dressed in his warmest clothes, and
followed Fledermaus out onto the balcony.

The world had been transformed
overnight. Yesterday, the Mouse Islands

3

had been grey and brown and green. Now everything was sparkling white. The roofs of all the mouse houses were white.

Even the sea was white. The sky was grey,
but white things were falling out of it.
LOTS of fluffy white things!

One of them landed on Pedro's nose and perched there, making his whiskers tingle. It was a tiny, perfect snowflake.

SPLOOF! went a much larger white thing, whooshing past Pedro's ear and hitting Fledermaus full in the face.

Down below, the other Adventure-mice were scrambling over the rocks around their harbour. Juniper shouted, 'Got you, Fledermaus!' and Fledermaus laughed, scooped some snow off the balcony rail, and moulded it into another snowball to throw back at her.

It looked such fun down there that Pedro was eager to join in. He ran to the stairs at the end of the balcony. But somebody seemed to have covered the stairs with glass. '**EEK!**' he squeaked, slipping over.

he added, bouncing down the slippery
stairs on his bottom. When he reached
the foot of the stairs it turned out that the
rocks below were just as slippery.

'Oh no!' Pedro squealed, slithering

across them. 'Help!' he squeaked,
dropping off the edge. 'Mouse overboard!'
he shouted, as he plunged towards the sea.

But instead of splashing into the water
he just went sliding across it on his tummy.
When he finally came to a stop and looked
back, all the Adventuremice had gathered
on the Mousebase harbour to watch him.

It was turning into a very confusing
sort of day.

'What's happened to the sea?' asked
Pedro, trying to get up and slipping over
again.

'It's frozen!' shouted Bosun. 'The ice

came early this year. The sea between the
Mouse Islands doesn't usually freeze over
till midwinter.'

Millie and Juniper jumped down onto
the frozen sea and started sliding out to
help Pedro. They didn't seem to have any
trouble standing up at all, and they sped

towards him very quickly and gracefully.
They had strapped little blades of metal
to their feet, which let them move about
easily on the ice.

'You are so good at this!' said Pedro, as
they helped him up and guided him back
to shore, one holding him by each paw.

'Of course we are!' said Millie. 'We are
Adventuremice, and Adventuremice are
prepared for anything.'

'You'll be good at it
too,' promised Juniper.
'We'll teach you
how to skate.'

'I've never been out in the snow and ice before,' said Pedro.

'Oh, it's lovely when you get used to it!' said Juniper. 'Everything is so pretty when it's just snowed.'

'And there's the Frost Fair!' said Millie. 'Pedro is going to *love* the Frost Fair!'

'What's the Frost Fair?' asked Pedro.

'It happens on Midwinter's Day, between Big Island and Bramble Isle,' said Millie. 'It's the most wonderful time of the whole year! Everyone puts their skates on and goes out onto the ice, and there are stalls and races and music and hot chocolate. And the Frost Fair Organizing Committee bring all sorts of marvellous treats from the mainland.'

'And don't forget the snowmouse competition!' said Fledermaus, reaching down to help Pedro ashore. 'I want our snowmouse to win first prize this year.'

'We'd better teach Pedro how to build a snowmouse!' said Ivy. 'A proper one, with

a scarf and one of Bosun's old hats and pebbles for eyes and a baby carrot for a nose.'

But Skipper, the leader of the Adventuremice, came buzzing over on his snowmobile just then to say, 'Sorry, Ivy! There's no time for making snowmice. We have a very serious problem on our paws . . .'

CHAPTER 2

TREATS

Pedro took extra special care not to slip as
he and the other Adventuremice followed
Skipper to the far side of the island. A
little group of mice had just arrived at
the entrance to the frozen Mousebase
harbour. They had come over the sea on
their skates, and were huddled together,
looking terribly worried.

'These mice are the Frost Fair

Organizing Committee,' said Skipper.

'And they've got some terrible news.'

The Adventuremice all listened very

solemnly as the leader of the committee

said, 'Our chairmouse, Wobbly Jeff,

sailed off with his helpers to the mainland

yesterday. There's a human café on the

shore where they get all the cheese and chocolate and other special treats for Frost Fair. But the sea froze before they came back! They must be stranded there!'

'That's terrible!' gasped Juniper. 'We'll have to rescue them!'

'But my seaplane is stuck in the ice too,' said Fledermaus.

'And my helicopter can't fly all the way to the mainland and back,' said Millie.

'And what about all the treats Wobbly Jeff went to fetch?' said Bosun. 'We'd need a ship to bring them back in.'

'Can't we take the *Daring Dormouse*?' said Pedro proudly. He was sure the Adventuremouse ship could cope with a bit of ice.

'Even the *Daring Dormouse* can't tackle ice this thick, Pedro,' said Ivy.

'Frost Fair won't be Frost Fair without treats,' said Bosun sadly. 'I've been looking forward to those special Frost Fair

chocolate pieces all year.'

'And spicy raisins . . .' said Skipper.

'And cheese snowflakes . . .' said Ivy.

'And toasted hazelnuts,' said Juniper.

'And sugar cubes,' said Fledermaus wistfully.

'I suppose we'll just have to face it,'
said Millie. 'Frost Fair is cancelled, and
Wobbly Jeff and his helpers will be stuck
on the mainland till the ice thaws.'

The Adventuremice all looked sad,
and Pedro felt very upset. He had never
seen his friends defeated before. He had
thought there was no problem in the world

that the Adventuremice couldn't solve.

Then he looked at the skates still strapped to Juniper and Millie's feet, and realized they might be able to solve this problem after all. A little nervously, he raised a paw.

'This is just a thought,' he said, 'and you'll probably say it's a silly idea. But what if we put skates on the *Daring Dormouse*?'

'You're right, Pedro,' said Fledermaus. 'It *is* a silly idea.'

But Ivy said, 'What do you mean, Pedro?'

'Well,' said Pedro bashfully, 'if we could make some really big skates, and get the *Daring Dormouse* out of the ice, and stick the skates underneath her, she could just slide across the ice to the mainland and bring back Wobbly Jeff and his helpers and all the Frost Fair treats.'

Skipper nodded thoughtfully. 'It's a long shot, but it might just work . . .'

Ivy said, 'We can't use the *Daring Dormouse*. She pushes herself through the water with her propeller, and that

wouldn't be much use on ice. We'd need a
sailing ship that the wind can push along.'

The littlest of the committee mice
raised her paw. 'There's an old sailing
ship at the boatyard on Little Dithering.
It isn't stuck in the ice because they pulled
it up out of the water last week. Maybe
you could put skates on that?'

'Not skates,' said Ivy. 'Skis! Great
big skis, strong enough to carry us and
Wobbly Jeff and his helpers and a whole

shipload of chocolate bars and cheese and nuts . . .'

'And don't forget the sugar cubes!' added Fledermaus.

Skipper clapped his paws together. 'Millie and Ivy, you fly over to Little Dithering in the helicopter and tell the shipyard mice to start work on some really massive skis!'

'Skis!' said Millie, excitedly. 'You're so clever, Ivy! And Pedro is a very quick-thinking mouse. Thanks to you, Frost Fair will be saved!'

CHAPTER 3
THE ICE SHIP

Millie's helicopter took off, with Ivy waving from the passenger seat, while the rest of the Adventuremice strapped on their skates and set off across the sea ice.

Pedro found skating quite difficult at first – the skates kept going backwards while he was going forwards, and he

would end up in
a heap on the
ice. But the other
Adventuremice helped
him up and patiently
showed him what to
do. By the time they had
skated all the way to
Little Dithering
he was starting to get
quite good at it.
As they neared
the boatyard they
could hear the sounds

of hammering
echoing out
across the frozen
sea. The ship was
standing at the top
of the slipway, held
upright by scaffolding.
She was an old wooden ship
and her figurehead was carved
in the shape of a beautiful mouse
holding up an even more beautiful
wedge of cheese. Her name was the
Cheddar Princess.

'She was the fastest cheese clipper in

the Mouse Islands

in her time,' said Mr

McWhiskers the shipwright,

coming out of his workshop to greet the

Adventuremice. 'She made lots of daring

voyages to the mainland, and came home

with her holds stuffed full of cheddar, brie

and stilton. But nowadays electric cheese-freighters can do the trip in half the time. I was repairing the old girl so I could use her for pleasure trips round Dithering Bay. But your friend Ivy seems to think she has one more voyage in her . . .'

Ever since she was a little mouselet, Ivy had loved working out what made things go, and fixing them when they were broken. It was she who

had designed all the Adventuremice ships
and aircraft. As soon as
she saw the *Cheddar
Princess* she knew
what must be done.
By the time the rest
of the Adventuremice
arrived, she and Millie
and the shipyard mice
were busy making
two enormous skis. They
made them from old
boat trailers and packing
crates and whatever

32

else they could find. When they needed metal struts to attach the skis to the *Cheddar Princess*, Skipper and the others scurried along to the nearby playground and uprooted the climbing frame.

Nobody minded, because the local
mouselets were all too busy sledging and
having snowball fights to use the climbing
frame today, and Ivy promised that she
would make them a new one before the
snow thawed.

All day they worked, and long into the night. When next morning came, it found the snow deeper than ever, the sea ice even thicker, and the *Cheddar Princess* standing proudly but a little uncertainly on her new skis at the top of the slipway.

The Adventuremice climbed aboard.
One of the committee mice passed up
a map for Skipper. 'Wobbly Jeff always
collects the treats from the same place. It's
called the Waterside Café,' she explained.

'Will it be dangerous?' asked Pedro.
'Are there any dogs or cats at this
Waterside Café?'

'The café is guarded by a cat called Tiger,' said the committee mouse. 'He sounds fierce, but actually he's old and lazy and no danger at all. The humans who eat at the café all give him bits of their fish fingers and tuna sandwiches, so he can't be bothered to chase mice.'

That sounded good to Pedro. But he was still worried about the *Cheddar Princess*. The old ship looked so strange, perched on her skis. What if she tipped over? What if she was too heavy and the ice broke underneath her? What if she would not move at all?

But all around him the other Adventuremice were preparing to set off. Bosun stood at the ship's wheel, Millie and Juniper scrambled about in the rigging, and Ivy ran around making last-minute checks on the skis.

'Hoist sails!' commanded Skipper, and Pedro ran to help Fledermaus pull on one of the ropes which raised the massive mainsail.

Soon all was ready. The mayoress of Little Dithering broke a bottle of mouse lemonade against the *Cheddar Princess*'s bows and said, 'I name this ice ship the

Cheddar Princess, and jolly good luck to all who sail in her.' Then Mr McWhiskers and his shipyard mice and the Frost Fair Organizing Committee all got behind the old ship and pushed. The *Cheddar Princess* went slithering swiftly down the slipway and onto the ice.

The ice did not break. It creaked a little as it took the *Cheddar Princess*'s weight, but it held, and the ship went gliding out across the frozen bay.

The snow had stopped falling, and a cold wind had sprung up. Unfortunately it was blowing from the east, which was the direction the *Cheddar Princess* wanted to be blown in. She really needed a nice west wind to blow her to the Waterside Café. With the wind blowing straight towards her, she slowly slid to a stop. But Bosun said, 'Never mind. If this east wind holds, it'll be just right for bringing us home when we've found Wobbly Jeff and stuffed the ship full of gingerbread and cheese snowflakes and chocolate-biscuit crumbs . . .'

'Don't forget the sugar cubes,' shouted

Fledermaus, from the top of a mast.

Then Bosun showed them how to turn the sails so that the wind filled them. The *Cheddar Princess* began to move again. She was moving in the wrong direction, but that didn't bother Bosun.

'We'll go south-east for a bit,' he said. 'Then we'll swing the sails around and head north-east. We'll keep doing that, and each time we turn we'll be a little further east. It's called tacking, and it's how sailing ships move when the wind isn't being helpful. Ready about!'

'That means, "get ready to turn",' said

Millie, and Pedro ducked just in time as
the sails all swung round. The *Cheddar
Princess* turned until she was pointing
north-east. This was going to take ages,

thought Pedro. But at least they were moving. They were already quite a long way from the shipyard, heading in slow zig-zags for the mainland.

'Hurrah!' shouted the shipyard mice and the Organizing Committee and all the mice of Little Dithering, who had turned out to watch. 'Hurrah! Frost Fair is saved! Goodbye, Adventuremice! Good luck! Come back soon!'

CHAPTER 4

MICE ON THE ICE

All day the *Cheddar Princess* made her slow way east, and sometimes it snowed on her and sometimes it didn't. She sailed past other mouse islands, where mice on skates and skis and sleds came scudding out to wave and watch her pass. She sailed past the Mousebase, and the Adventuremice

all felt a little homesick as it dwindled
behind them, but they were all much too
brave to mention it. They sailed past a
few stuck mouse ships, wedged tight in the
ice. Skipper called to the stranded crews
through his loudhailer, promising them

that as soon as the *Cheddar Princess* came home he would send Millie to collect them in her helicopter so they would not miss the Frost Fair.

Around lunchtime, one of the skis started making a sort of grumbly noise. It was coming loose! Skipper ordered the sails to be lowered, and the ship slid to a stop in the midst of a big, white, icy nothing.

While Ivy and Fledermaus climbed down onto the ski and started repairing it, Pedro noticed something on the ice nearby.

'It's a crab,' said Skipper, looking at it through his telescope. 'Poor thing! It ought to be down underwater. It must have got stuck on the surface when the freeze came.'

'Can we help it?' asked Pedro.

'That would delay us,' said Skipper. 'And crabs can be dangerous, with those great big pincers of theirs.'

'My Auntie Myrtle was nipped by a crab,' said Bosun, 'and she was never the same again.'

But the other Adventuremice said, 'Of course we must help it! We are Adventuremice!'

As soon as the repairs were finished they all strapped on their skates and set out across the ice to where the poor crab sat shivering. They went very slowly and cautiously, but the crab's pincers were

shaking so much that it couldn't have
nipped them even if it had wanted to.

'I don't like this hard sort of sea
they have nowadays,' the poor crab
grumbled. 'Call me unsophisticated, but
I preferred the old-fashioned wet sort of
sea. I've been sitting out here on this cold,

hard stuff for ages, and you're the first
other creatures I've seen. What are you
anyway? Some sort of dry land animals I
suppose. Rhinoceroses perhaps. Or maybe
aardvarks.'

'We're mice!' laughed the Adventuremice.

'Is that so? I don't know very much
about dry land animals, you see; it was all

sealife around these parts until they went and installed this new-fangled hard sea. I live underwater myself. Oh, I do so wish I could get back there. My family will be wondering where I've got to.'

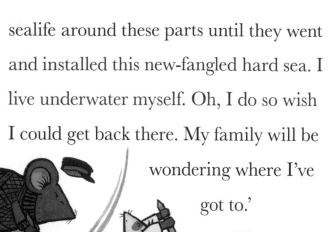

The Adventuremice told him not to worry; they would soon get him home. Then they set to work with pickaxes and saws and Ivy's welding torch. They chipped and cut and melted the

ice until they had made a big hole in it. In
the hole, open water sloshed and sploshed.

'Hurry up!' they told the crab. 'Before
it freezes over again!'

Two big tears of happiness filled the
crab's eyes and trickled down their stalks.

'You are very kind creatures,' he said. 'You are quite the kindest aardvarks I have ever met.'

'We're MICE!' yelled the Adventuremice, but the crab had already scuttled over to the hole they'd made for him and plopped into the water. 'Goodbye, aardvarks!' he said, waving a grateful pincer, and sank into the depths.

The Adventuremice skated back to where the *Cheddar Princess* waited. They felt happy and pleased with themselves, for they had helped the crab, and helping is what Adventuremice are all about. But

cutting that crab-sized hole had taken
longer than they had expected. Already
the short winter day was dying, and the
reds and golds of
a cold sunset

glowed in the western sky.

All through the night the *Cheddar Princess* sailed on beneath the frosty stars. Pedro kept watch at the masthead, feeling very sleepy, and shivering despite his warmest jumper. All he could see was the starlit ice, and the two dark lines the ship's skis had drawn across it, vanishing away behind her. It felt very lonely to be a small mouse in such a vast, cold world. But towards morning, Ivy came climbing up the rigging with a mug of hot chocolate and a toast crumb for him, and then he didn't feel lonely any more.

'This is the life!' said Ivy, sitting down beside him. 'Making things work is such fun, and I'm so glad we were able to help that silly crab get home. And look! There's land ahead! Will you tell the others, or shall I?'

Pedro looked out into the greyness of the coming day. Sure enough, there were the snow-covered hills of the mainland. He gulped his hot chocolate down, sprang to his feet, and shouted in his most important voice, 'Land ho! Land on the starboard bow!'

The land on the starboard bow was the beach where the Waterside Café stood, and there was the café itself. It was all shut up and dark, because it wouldn't be opening for another hour or more. Pedro stared at it as Bosun guided the *Cheddar Princess* into the shadows under a nearby jetty. He had got so used to mouse-sized buildings during his time among the islands that a human-sized building looked unbelievably huge.

'How on earth are we going to find what we need in a place that big?' he wondered.

'We'll follow our noses, of course,' said Skipper. 'I can already smell those spicy raisins.'

'And Wobbly Jeff will help,' said Juniper. 'Look! That must be him and his helpers!'

Three mice had run down to the

water's edge beneath the jetty. They
were jumping up and down and waving
their paws to attract the attention of the
Adventuremice. As the *Cheddar Princess*
came to a stop they jumped onto her

bowsprit and ran along it onto the deck.

'Thank you for coming!' squeaked the leader of the mice. He was a plump old sailormouse with white whiskers, and he had spent so much of his life at sea that he always wobbled a bit when he was on dry land – that was how he had got his name. 'I'm Wobbly Jeff,' he said, 'and these fine young mouselets are my helpers, Twitch and Ida.'

'We knew the Adventuremice would save us!' said Twitch.

'Where is your ship?' asked Bosun.

'There!' said Wobbly Jeff, and pointed sadly into the shadows beneath the jetty. There was the ship, or what was left of it – the ice had crushed it almost flat.

'Let's get the treats out and bring them aboard the *Cheddar Princess*,' said Skipper. 'Then we'll head for home.'

Wobbly Jeff and his helpers looked nervously at one another. Ida raised a paw. 'There aren't any treats,' she said. 'We weren't able to get any this year.'

'Why not?' asked Fledermaus. 'The café is right there. Mmm, I can smell those spiced raisins from here!'

'We tried,' said Wobbly Jeff. 'But it was too dangerous! We barely escaped with our lives! There is a terrible cat inside the café!'

'Tiger?' asked Pedro. 'I thought he was too full of leftovers to bother with mice.'

'Oh, he is!' agreed Wobbly Jeff. 'In years gone by we

always ran right over him, carrying
whole sandwiches we'd borrowed from
the kitchen. Sleepy old Tiger would just
open one eye and look at us and then go
on snoring. But that was the trouble, you
see. It made us too greedy. We helped
ourselves to biscuits, bits of cheese,
whole muffins . . .' He sighed wistfully,
remembering those golden days.

'Eventually the humans who own the café noticed what was going on. And that was when it happened.'

'When what happened?' asked the Adventuremice.

'They got another cat!' said Ida.

Twitch shuddered.

'This new one is called . . . *Fluffykins*.'

'What a cute name!' said Millie.

'Oh, there's nothing cute about Fluffykins!' said Wobbly Jeff. 'She's a lean, mean, mouse-hunting machine.'

The Adventuremice didn't like the sound of that.

'What do you think, Skipper?' asked Ivy. 'Is it too dangerous?'

Skipper looked up at the café and shook his head. 'It will be risky,' he said, 'and we must be very, very careful. But we haven't come all this way just to go back empty-pawed.'

'Three cheers for the Adventuremice!' shouted Fledermaus. 'Hip, hip . . .'

'Shhhh!' said Wobbly Jeff. 'Fluffykins
will hear you! Her ears are just as sharp as
her claws and her teeth.'

'Hurrah!' cheered the Adventuremice,
in tiny whispers.

They gathered up the bags and sacks
they had brought to transport the treats.
Skipper went into his cabin, and came
out buckling on his sword.

'Fluffykins isn't the only one

with sharp claws,' he said, patting its hilt. Pedro remembered the stories he had heard about how Skipper had once fought a cat and won. He began to feel a little braver.

Bosun lowered the gangplank. The Adventuremice all scurried ashore, leaving Wobbly Jeff and his helpers to mind the ship.

Wobbly Jeff had drawn a map for them, showing the layout of the café and the best place to get in. Skipper led the way past the closed front door and along the outside of the building to where a mousehole opened into the storeroom. While the others waited nervously outside, he crept in alone to check that Fluffykins wasn't on the prowl. After a moment he returned.

'There are no cats in the storeroom,' he said. 'Just

DOOR

boxes and boxes of treats. Come on!'

The others followed him inside. The
storeroom was quite small for human
beings, but to the Adventuremice it
seemed enormous; a shadowy cavern

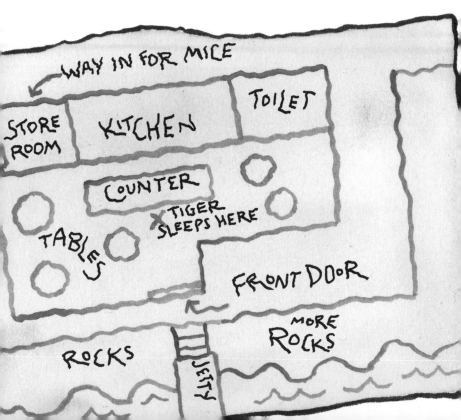

WAY IN FOR MICE

STORE ROOM

KITCHEN

TOILET

COUNTER

TIGER SLEEPS HERE

TABLES

FRONT DOOR

MORE ROCKS

ROCKS

JETTY

crammed with cardboard boxes of delights. Bosun tore his way into one of the cartons and Ivy and Skipper helped him drag out three big chocolate bars in shiny wrappers – enough to provide plenty of chocolate crumbs for everyone at the Frost Fair. Millie and Juniper climbed up to one of the higher shelves and found raisins, crisps, and pieces of crystallized ginger,

which the other mice packed quickly into their bags. They dragged everything back outside and down under the jetty to where the *Cheddar Princess* waited. When the bags were stowed safely in the ice ship's hold they ran back to make a second raid on the storeroom. By the time that haul was all safely packed away the *Cheddar Princess*'s hold looked almost full.

'I think that's enough treats for half a dozen Frost Fairs,' said Pedro proudly.

'But we have to visit the storeroom one more time,' said Fledermaus. 'We haven't found any sugar cubes yet!'

'There will be some in the café,' said Wobbly Jeff. 'The humans keep a bowl full of sugar cubes on the middle of each table.'

'Let's not push our luck,' warned Bosun. 'We don't want to wake up Fluffykins.'

But Skipper said, 'I'm partial to sugar cubes too. The rest of you stay here and make the ship ready to leave. Fledermaus, Pedro – you come with me.'

CHAPTER 6

FLUFFYKINS

Back they ran to the café. Once inside, they crept underneath the storeroom door and tiptoed out into the café itself. It was dark in there, because the blinds on the windows were still pulled down. In the shadows, huge chairs and tables loomed over the three mice like city buildings.

'Look!' whispered Pedro, pointing.

On a warm patch of lino ahead of them lay something huge and hairy and marmalade-coloured. It was a cat, sound asleep and snoring. Skipper motioned for Pedro and Fledermaus to stay back while he went to take a closer look.

'It's all right,' he whispered. 'I can read its name tag from here. This cat is Tiger, and he's just as sleepy as everyone says.'

Tiger went on snoring while the three mice scurried up the leg of the nearest table. On the top of the table stood a bowl filled with white and brown sugar cubes.

While Pedro and Fledermaus quickly
filled their sacks (and nibbled a few of the
sugar cubes just to test that they were good
ones) Skipper looked around. He had a
twitchy feeling in his whiskers that told
him danger was near.

In the shadows at the far end of the café two small, round lights had come on.

Two small, round, yellow lights, with black slits down their middles.

Two small, round, yellow lights that looked almost like . . .

'CAT'S EYES!' shouted Skipper.

'Mrawwwwr!' roared Fluffykins.

The mice scattered as a sleek black cat sprang at them. If Pedro hadn't jumped off the table just in time he would have been eaten in a single gulp. He heard Fluffykins's jaws shut with a snap just above him as he dropped to the floor.

Up on the tabletop, Skipper drew his
sword. Fluffykins swung round
to attack him, just in time to
get poked on the nose by the
sharp point.

She sprang

backwards so

violently that the table fell over, spilling Skipper and Fledermaus onto the floor. Fluffykins got tangled in the tablecloth, and by the time she had clawed her way out all three mice were running at top speed towards the storeroom door. Fluffykins hissed with rage and sprang after them, but they squeezed under the door before she could catch them.

While angry claws raked at the door
behind them, the mice scurried across the
storeroom and out through the hole in the
wall. There they stopped, panting, their
breath making smoky clouds in the cold air.

'What about the sugar cubes?' asked
Fledermaus. 'I dropped my sack in all the
kerfuffle.'

'So did I,' said Pedro.

'You know, I've gone off the idea of sugar cubes,' said Skipper.

'I've heard they're very bad for you,' agreed Fledermaus.

'Mrawwwwr!' said Fluffykins, popping out suddenly through a flap in the bottom of the café door. She sprang towards the three Adventuremice.

'Ivy! Bosun!' yelled Skipper. 'We are leaving!' He drew his sword and prepared to fight while Pedro and Fledermaus ran down to where the *Cheddar Princess* was waiting. But Fluffykins hung back, wary of the icy ground and afraid of being pricked again by Skipper's sharp little blade. When Pedro and Fledermaus had climbed aboard the ship, Skipper turned and scampered after them. The other Adventuremice had already raised the ship's sails by the time he jumped aboard. But the ship wasn't moving.

'There's no wind under here!' shouted

Ivy. 'We'll have to push the *Princess* further out!'

The Adventuremice jumped down onto the ice. So did Wobbly Jeff and his helpers. They all put their paws against the *Cheddar Princess*'s skis and pushed for all they were worth.

Slowly the ship started to edge out from under the jetty, into the wind.

Meanwhile, Fluffykins prowled along the jetty, very displeased by the cold, wet snow under her paws. As she reached the jetty's end she saw the *Cheddar Princess* appear, with a whole crowd of mice pushing her along. Fluffykins laid back her ears. Her eyes shone with a hungry light. All her muscles tensed, ready to spring.

Down on the ice, the sails of the *Cheddar Princess* finally filled with the wind. It was blowing nice and strongly and in just the right direction, but it still wasn't enough to move the ship very fast.

'She's too heavy!' said Bosun, as they scrambled back aboard. The *Cheddar Princess* was sliding across the ice a little slower than a mouse could walk.

'It's all those treats!' said Ivy. 'They're weighing us down!'

'It will take us days and days to reach the Mouse Islands at this speed,' grumbled Millie.

'But we don't have days and days!' said Pedro. 'Because LOOK!'

Fluffykins sprang off the end of the jetty and landed on the ice. She hated ice, but she hated mice even more. Slipping and slithering, she started to creep after the *Cheddar Princess*.

'There's nothing else for it,' decided Skipper. 'Empty the hold!'

The Adventuremice started running down to the hold and running back up with the bags of treats they'd stowed there. Maybe if they threw just half of the treats overboard the ship would move fast enough to escape from Fluffykins? But no, the cat was still gaining on them. Desperately, they started to throw the rest of the treats away too.

The *Cheddar Princess* still wasn't moving at top speed, but she was getting faster. She skated over a patch of thin ice, which creaked and cracked beneath her skis.

'Maybe Fluffykins will fall through the ice!' said Fledermaus hopefully. 'It only just took our weight, and a cat must be much heavier than us . . .'

But Fluffykins was getting the hang of walking on the ice. When she reached the thin place and the ice cracked beneath her paws she simply jumped across it, and landed on firmer ice in front of the ship. Her tail twitched eagerly to and fro as she crouched there wondering which Adventuremouse to gobble up first.

But before she could decide, something

scrambled up out of the crack she had made in the ice and grabbed the tip of Fluffykins's tail. She screeched and spun around.

A big crab was hanging on to her tail by his pincers.

'Hello, my aardvark friends!' the crab said, as Fluffykins's frantic whirling swung him past the startled Adventuremice. 'One good turn deserves another! But I don't think I can hang on to this strange animal for long. You'd better get away while you can!'

The Adventuremice heaved a last, heavy bag of hazelnuts overboard. The *Cheddar Princess* began to pick up speed, gliding away towards the far-off islands.

'Goodbye! Thank you!' shouted the Adventuremice, waving from the stern

and then running up the masts to keep on waving. They waved until they were out of sight, while the crab waved back, still clinging on tight to Fluffykins's tail with the other pincer.

At last, Fluffykins decided she had had enough. With a final, disgusted hiss she turned tail and went running back towards the café. The crab let go of her and dropped down onto the ice, which was covered in raisins, chocolate bars, pieces of ginger, and all sorts of other treats.

'Ooh, presents!' said the crab, and started shoving the things towards the ice hole, where they would sink down to his family's underwater home. 'They really are the most kind and thoughtful aardvarks!'

He waved a pincer towards the west. But the Adventuremice were gone, and all he could see were the marks of the *Cheddar Princess*'s skis vanishing over the horizon.

CHAPTER 7

THE FROST FAIR

The Frost Fair Organizing Committee were waiting at the Mousebase when the Adventuremice came home. They cheered, and waved little flags, and unfurled a banner that said:

WELCOME HOME, BRAVE TREAT FETCHERS!

Frankly, the Adventuremice rather wished they hadn't bothered.

For how were they to break the news that they'd had to abandon their precious cargo? How were they to explain that the Frost Fair was cancelled after all?

'It is all my fault,' said Ivy. 'I should have allowed for the extra weight of the cargo. I knew we would move more slowly on the way home, but I didn't think it mattered.'

'You weren't to know we'd meet that cat,' said Skipper. 'The fault is mine. If I hadn't been greedy and decided to go looking for sugar cubes . . .'

In the end it was Pedro who ran to
the tip of the ship's bowsprit and told the
waiting mice what had happened.

The mice stopped waving their flags.
Their banner drooped. 'So you haven't
brought any treats . . . at all?' they sniffled.

Pedro led them aboard and took them down into the hold. It was empty, except for a single hazelnut and a solitary chocolate bar.

'But we thought you'd bring back everything we need for Frost Fair!' said one of the mice, stifling a sob.

'Well the adventure didn't quite work out this time,' said Pedro. 'All we brought back were this hazelnut and this bar of chocolate and a nail-biting story.'

'There is a new cat at the café,' explained Wobbly Jeff. 'It very nearly ate us all up!'

The committee mice had baked some Welcome Home With All The Treats cookies, and it seemed a shame to waste them, so they passed them around and

sat listening with wide eyes and trembling whiskers while the Adventuremice told the tale of their strange voyage and their narrow escape.

When it was finished, the leader of the committee said, 'Well, it sounds as if we're lucky you came back at all! And Frost Fair isn't just about treats, is it? It's about seeing friends and being with your family and telling stories and playing games. Will you come and tell the story of your adventure at Frost Fair?'

'Oh, we can do better than that!' said Skipper. 'These cookies are excellent, and they have given me an idea. Most mice have got enough bits and pieces in their larders to make some cakes or some cookies or some sandwiches. They won't be the usual Frost Fair treats, but at least they will be something.'

'I'll go and bake one of my special cakes!' said Bosun.

'And the rest of us will tell all the mice of the Mouse Islands to bring something nice to share at the Frost Fair!' said Ivy.

So they did. All that day and all the next the *Cheddar Princess* went sliding from one Mouse Island to the next. Wherever she stopped, the mice came out to see Ivy's marvellous new ship, and the Adventuremice told them to get making and baking.

The day of the Frost Fair dawned crisp and bright, and the frozen sea between Nibbleton and Bramble Isle was covered with stalls and tables where mice could swap homemade cakes and cookies, tasty pies, toasty peas, hazelnut bakes, and bowls of bramble soup. The chocolate bar that the Adventuremice had brought home was broken up into so many tiny bits that there was one for everybody, and two for Fledermaus and Pedro, the winners of the snowmouse competition. Everyone agreed that the *Cheddar Princess* was Ivy's cleverest invention yet, and they queued up to take

rides on her around the bay. (Ivy said she
was Pedro's idea really, but everyone knew
the idea couldn't have been turned into a
real ice ship without Ivy.)

And even when all the food had been
eaten, the games and stories went on, long

into the night, while the stars twinkled like fairy lights, and the fairy lights twinkled like stars.

'It's the best Frost Fair ever!' said Pedro.

'How do you know?' asked Fledermaus. 'This is the first Frost Fair you've been to.'

'I can just tell it's the best,' said Pedro.

And the Adventuremice all knew he was right.

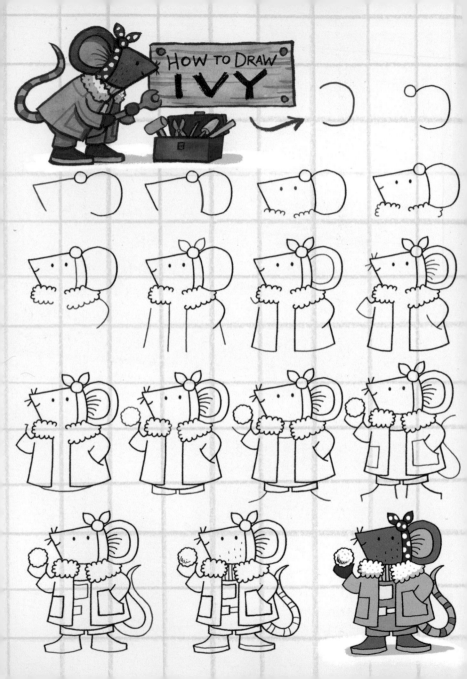

HOW TO DRAW
IVY

ABOUT THE AUTHORS

SARAH McINTYRE

LOVES DRAWING MORE THAN WRITING. BUT SHE OFTEN HELPS HER CO-AUTHOR PHILIP WITH THE WORDS WHEN HE WANTS SOME NEW IDEAS.

PHILIP REEVE

LOVES WRITING MORE THAN DRAWING. BUT HE HELPS SARAH WITH THE PICTURES SO THEY WON'T TAKE QUITE SO LONG TO MAKE.

THEY BOTH LOVE BEACHES, DRIFTWOOD AND THE SEA, AND MAKING UP STORIES ABOUT MYSTERIOUS ISLANDS.